NEW CLOTHES FOR ALEX

Mary Dickinson

Pictures by Charlotte Firmin

Hippo Books
Scholastic Publications Limited
London

Scholastic Publications Ltd.,
10 Earlham Street, London WC2H 9RX, UK

Scholastic Inc.,
730 Broadway, New York, NY 10003, USA

Scholastic Tab Publications Ltd.,
123 Newkirk Road, Richmond Hill,
Ontario L4C 3G5, Canada

Ashton Scholastic Pty. Ltd.,
PO Box 579, Gosford, New South Wales,
Australia

Ashton Scholastic Ltd.,
165 Marua Road, Panmure, Auckland 6,
New Zealand

First published by André Deutsch Limited, 1984

Published in paperback by
Scholastic Publications Ltd., 1985
Text copyright © Mary Dickinson, 1984
Illustrations copyright © Charlotte Firmin, 1984
Reprinted 1986

ISBN 0 590 70446 X

"Alex! I can see your tummy," said his mother.

"It looks as if I need to buy you some new clothes."

"No you don't," said Alex, pulling down his sweater.

"Yes I do," argued his mother. "You've grown very tall lately."

"I don't want to go shopping," said Alex crossly. "It's such a long way to the shops."

"You could ride your bike," suggested his mother.

Alex grinned. "And have a cake?"

"Yes; if there's any money left."

Alex's mother grabbed her shopping bag and they set off for the shops at once; just in case Alex changed his mind.

Alex rode his bike as fast as he could. His mother had to run to keep up with him.

"I don't think this was a very good idea after all," she puffed.

"I want to go home," Alex said as soon as they reached the shops. "There's too many people here. Someone is sure to tread on me."

"Of course they won't," said his mother. "And we're not going home till I've bought you some new clothes."

"I won't wear them," growled Alex, giving his mother his very fierce monster stare.

To his surprise she growled back!

Alex's mother went over to a shop window. "Do you like any of those T-shirts or sweaters, Alex?"
"No," said Alex.

They moved to the next window.
"Do you like any of those shoes?"
"No," said Alex.

They moved to another window.

"What about those trousers?"

"Yuk, they're horrible," answered Alex.

"Oh Alex," his mother said sharply. "Where am I going to find something you like?"

Just then she noticed a big department store. "Oh, that would be a good place to look, Alex. It's where I bought the clothes you've got on. Come on." She pulled Alex into the store.

The children's clothes department was upstairs. Alex's mother asked the security man to look after Alex's bike so that they could ride upstairs on the escalator.

"I do like the escalator," said Alex.

"So do I," sighed his mother. "It gives my legs a rest."

The children's department was very big and very busy. Alex's mother wondered where they should look first. Suddenly Alex screamed, "Ooouch, oooooh. MUM. Mum, that great big silly old body trod on me. Told you someone would. Can we go home now?"
"Shhh," said his mother kindly. "I'll carry you if you like."
She lifted him onto her shoulders. "Oh Alex," she groaned, "you've grown very heavy."

"It's good up here," said Alex, forgetting all about his squashed foot. "I can see everything. There's some good clothes over there, Mum."

Alex's mother clumped and swayed over to where Alex was pointing. Alex had to hold on very tightly. She laughed when she saw the clothes. "I'll buy them if they fit you," she promised.

Alex tried them on in a special changing room. The clothes fitted so they bought them.

After she had paid, Alex's mother looked into her purse. "I've got some money left. You can have your cake, Alex."

Alex chose a cake that looked like a traffic light.
His mother's cake was filled with cream.
They stopped by the pond to eat them.
The ducks looked at Alex so sadly that he gave them half his cake.
"It was a very sticky cake," said Alex wiping his hands down his trousers.
"Oh Alex," said his mother. "Now you will have to change into your new clothes when we get home."

When they were at home, Alex took the things they had bought to his bedroom.
He took off his clothes and put them on his big teddy. Then he dressed himself in the new clothes.
"Look, Mum," he called.

Alex's mother peeped into his bedroom.
"Oh my goodness," she said. "You gave me
a fright. Just for a minute I thought I had two
Alexes!"

PRINTED IN BELGIUM BY

proost

INTERNATIONAL BOOK PRODUCTION